PARTY CRASHERS

BAKUGAN

BATTLE BRAWLERS

PARTY CRASHERS

BY TRACEY WEST

SCHOLASTIC INC.

NEW YORK   TORONTO   LONDON   AUCKLAND   SYDNEY

MEXICO CITY   NEW DELHI   HONG KONG   BUENOS AIRES

ISBN-13: 978-0-545-13118-6
ISBN-10: 0-545-13118-9

12 11 10 9 8 7 6 5 4 3 2 1   9 10 11 12 13 14/0

COVER ART BY ISIDRE MONES AND ROBERT ROPER
PRINTED IN THE U.S.A.
FIRST PRINTING, MAY 2009

ONE DAY, STRANGE CARDS STARTED RAINING ON THE WORLD . . .

Nobody knew where the cards came from. But everyone knew they were something special.

A boy named Dan, along with kids all over the world, used the cards to invent a new game called Bakugan. They soon discovered that the cards were packed with incredible powers from another world.

That other world — Vestroia — is the home to all of the Bakugan warriors. After the cards rained down, a hole opened up between Vestroia and Earth. This time, Bakugan warriors were sucked into the human world. They sought out Bakugan brawlers, and soon the brawlers and warriors were battling side by side.

But now there's a new brawler in town. His name is Masquerade, and he's dangerous. He uses the Doom Card when he battles. This sinister card sends the opponent's losing Bakugan into the terrible Doom Dimension.

For some mysterious reason, Masquerade's mission is to take down Dan and his friends. He's using other brawlers to do his dirty work. Dan doesn't care who Masquerade sends — he's always ready for a good brawl . . . and he's not going to lose!

CHAPTER 1

THE NEW KID IN TOWN

In the heart of the city, a shimmering glass skyscraper towered above the other buildings. The glass sparkled in shades of pink and orange under the bright afternoon sun.

On the very top of the building sat a small blue Bakugan ball. The ball opened up to reveal the head of a Preyas Bakugan with an Aquos attribute. He gazed out over the amazing view of the city. The blue water of the river flowed in the distance.

"Wow," said Preyas. "A penthouse with a view! Too bad the commute's a real killer."

A gray pigeon swooped down from up above.

"Hey, taxi!" Preyas cried. He jumped onto the pigeon's back. "Quick! To the flower bed below, and step on it!"

The pigeon didn't take orders from a Bakugan,

of course. It flew past the flower bed and across the city. . . .

In a yellow house not far away, Dan was hanging out with his friend Runo. She was on her computer, talking with Julie and Alice via videocam. Julie's blonde hair was piled into a ponytail. Alice had red hair and kind brown eyes.

At the bottom of her screen, Runo was clicking on photos of the skyscraper.

"Yeah, they sure are taking their time. But after six months of construction and two months of coffee breaks, we still don't know what it is," Runo said. "What could be taking so long to build?"

"Maybe a dance studio," Alice said.

"How about a fitness center and spa!" Julie suggested, her blue eyes shining.

Dan was lounging in a chair, reading a comic book. "I think you're making a big deal out of nothing," he said, looking up from the pages.

"It's *not* nothing!" Runo said. "If it's a mall or a giant coffee shop it could have disastrous effects on my parents' restaurant."

Runo flipped open the Baku-pod strapped to her wrist. "According to my market research calculations . . ."

"Ha! Market research?" Dan teased. "Don't make me laugh. You barely have customers, never mind a market."

Runo spun around on her chair, fuming. "You free-loading, ungrateful brat!"

Dan's Bakugan, Drago, and Runo's Bakugan, Tigrerra, perched on Runo's dresser, watched the scene.

"Dan! Just let this one go," Drago urged.

"This is one battle you won't win," Tigrerra agreed.

"It was just a joke!" Dan protested. "Don't freeze me out of the free snackage. I'm your best customer."

With perfect timing, Marucho's face popped up on Runo's computer screen.

"Hey, guys!" Marucho said cheerfully. The young boy had blonde hair and big eyeglasses. He wore a white and blue sailor shirt — the same kind of shirt he wore every day. "I just solved the skyscraper mystery."

"What?" Runo asked.

Marucho cleared his throat, like he was about to make some big announcement. "Turns out — it's my house!"

Runo, Dan, Alice, and Julie all groaned at the same time. They knew Marucho's family was rich, but they didn't know he was this rich.

"Yeah, I know. I was floored when my parents first

told me we were moving to your city," he said. "I kept it a secret so that I could tell you in person and see the look on your faces. And guess what? We're throwing a party, and you're all invited."

On the edge of the city, Preyas sat in a bird's nest on top of five eggs, sleeping peacefully. The nest was settled in the branches of a green tree in a stretch of woods along the roadside.

Preyas gave a yawn and woke up, opening up his Bakugan ball. He looked around him. He was far away from that luxury penthouse.

A tapping sound came from inside the eggs. Thin cracks appeared on the shells.

"Oh, no!" he cried. A beak poked out from one of the eggs. "Oh, no, no, no, no, no!"

Five baby birds poked out of the eggs now. Hungry, they chirped loudly.

"Silence! Silence! Evil five-headed monster!" Preyas cried.

He tried to balance on top of the pointy beaks, but it was no use. "Back off! I have weapons. What? Put down that stick! Stop pushing me! Aaaaaaaah!"

He tumbled out of the nest and rolled onto the ground. He went speeding down a hillside.

"Tuck and roll! Tuck and roll!" Preyas yelled. "Ouch! That was a rock!"

He reached the bottom of the hill and landed with a giant bounce. The bounce sent him flying into the bed of a passing truck. Luckily, he landed in a fancy display of flowers.

"I can't see! I can't see!" he yelled, trying to push the flowers aside. "Oh. It's a leaf!"

CHAPTER 2

MARUCHO'S RICHES

The next day, Runo and Dan walked down the street to Marucho's party. Runo, as usual, wore a stylishly funky outfit: a yellow crop top, white skirt, with white and orange striped socks. Her aqua ponytails bounced on her shoulders as she walked.

Dan wore his favorite red shirt and pants. His sunglasses were stuck on top of his head in a mop of wavy brown hair.

As they got near, they saw a long line of people standing in front of the skyscraper. Three stern-looking men in suits sat at a desk by the front door, checking everyone in.

Dan shielded his eyes from the sun and looked up at the glittering building. It was so tall he couldn't even see the top.

"Wow! This is his house?" Dan couldn't believe it.

"It must be so awesome to have so much money," Runo said dreamily. "With the parties, and the cars and the computers and the clothes . . . and the clothes."

"Yeah, and having people line up to get into your parties?" Dan said, frowning. "Come on, this is nuts. What kind of housewarming has a guest list and a bunch of posers waiting two hours to get in?"

Dan scanned the people on the line — and gasped. "What's my mom doing here? This is *so* not good!"

Marucho ran up to them, his face beaming with excitement. "Hi, Dan! Hi, Runo!"

"Hey Marucho," Dan said.

Runo smiled. "What's poppin'?"

"Hey, it's great to finally meet you in person!" Marucho chirped. He was only a couple of years younger than Dan and Runo, but half their size. "Like the new clothes?"

Marucho motioned to his blue and white sailor shirt and blue shorts.

"Uh, they kind of look like the ones you always wear," Runo said. "But you do look very nice."

A man and woman walked up behind Marucho.

"Marucho, are these your cyber friends?" asked the man. He had neatly combed hair, a mustache, and wore a suit. "I'm very pleased to meet you."

"We are his parents," said the woman, who had blonde hair just like Marucho's.

Dan and Runo bowed respectfully.

"Oh, hi!" Dan said. "Sorry I took up so much time on your dial-up. Welcome to the hood. I'm Dan."

"And I'm Runo," Runo said, a little nervously.

"No need to worry. We have the latest in fiber optics now," said Marucho's mom cheerfully.

"Yes, we upgraded everything thanks to a sweet land deal," said Marucho's dad. "In fact, Dan, your neighborhood was so cheap I nearly bought out the entire block. Ha!"

Dan wasn't sure if he should feel insulted or not. "Uh, yeah, cheap."

"Hey, Dad, can I give them a tour of our house?" Marucho asked. "I'll even do a preliminary security check."

Marucho's father nodded. "Sure. Knock yourselves out."

"Great," Marucho said. "Follow me."

Dan and Runo walked with Marucho past the security desk and into the mansion's front doors. They stepped into a huge room with marble floors and a high ceiling. Two staircases covered with red velvet led up to the second floor. Pots of beautiful flowers were lined up against the walls. A crowd of party guests was milling around the space.

Runo's turquoise eyes were wide with wonder. "This is so huge! We're talking major bling!"

"I know," Marucho said. "And my parents insist on basic cable. What's up with that?"

The three of them walked past the flower arrangements. Inside one of the flowers, a blue Bakugan ball opened up.

It was Preyas! The delivery truck had brought him exactly where he wanted.

"Ha!" Preyas said. "Now for Operation Magnum Stealth."

Preyas hurled himself out of the flowers and onto the floor — right into the path of traffic. A woman walked by and accidentally kicked him with her high heel.

"Ouch!" Preyas cried.

He rolled across the floor and bumped into another shoe. That sent him rocketing across the room like a ball in a pinball machine.

"Stop it! Stop it! Ouch! My shins!" Preyas wailed. "Aaaaaaah!"

Dan, Runo, and Marucho didn't know Preyas was in the building. They walked down one of the long, wide hallways of the mansion. They passed fancy doors with gold handles. Dan stopped in front of one of the doors.

"Is this your bedroom?" he asked, opening the door wide. He saw a big, round room with spotlights shining from the ceiling. "Whoa! This place is totally off the hook!"

"Uh, Dan, that's the bathroom," Marucho said.

Dan blinked. The spotlights shone on a gleaming white toilet bowl resting on an expensive rug. "Wow, even the toilet is tricked out."

He closed the door and they kept walking. They made a right turn into a hallway bathed in soft blue light. They took a few steps — and Dan and Runo gasped.

A gigantic blue whale swam by them, inside an enormous aquarium.

"WHAT?" Dan and Runo wondered.

"My mom likes to collect things like figurines — and endangered species," Marucho said, as if this were completely normal.

They stared at the blue whale and walked on. Beyond the aquarium, there was a huge indoor garden behind glass. Two giraffes peacefully munched on leaves. A round panda rested in the branches of a tree. Dan and Runo gaped in wonder.

And that wasn't all. The next room was an art gallery filled with famous artworks from all over the world. Finally, they stepped through two automatic sliding doors into Marucho's bedroom.

The whole room was as big as a basketball court. A chandelier shone overhead. One whole wall was taken up by a screen the size of a movie screen.

"Yes, it's big," Marucho admitted. "But in the middle of the night it's a bit of a trek just to get water."

Runo nodded to the screen. "Your plasma TV looks like a JumboTron from here."

"That's because it is," Marucho said. "Watch this."

He walked to a desk in the middle of the room. There was a complicated looking keyboard on the desk, and Marucho began typing on the keys. The big screen lit up — and Julie's face appeared.

"Hey guys!" she said. "That's a pretty cool trick you're doing, fitting onto one little screen like that instead of the multi screens. Technology is awesome!"

"Uh, maybe it's because we're all over at Marucho's house," Dan pointed out.

"What? Did someone forget to invite me? I thought you were supposed to call me, Runo!" Julie accused, her face turning red.

"Sorry," Runo said honestly. "I just like, totally forgot about it."

"Yeah, she's having trouble connecting the dots these days," Dan joked.

Runo poked Dan in the arm.

"Ow!" Dan cried.

Back downstairs, Preyas bounced from shoe to shoe until he reached the huge dining room. He bounced one final time and landed right in Dan's mom's purse. She walked out of the dining room and down one of the hallways.

"Which one of these is the bathroom?" she wondered. She opened the nearest door and found herself in a round room with mirrored walls. Built into the walls was a long counter covered with sparkling jewels.

Dan's mom gasped. "Are these for real?"

Preyas jumped out of the purse. He knew a good thing when he saw it. While Dan's mom stared, dazed at the gems, he wrapped a gold chain around one red ruby, one green emerald, and one sparkling diamond. Each round jewel was as big as he was.

Preyas began dragging the jewels across the floor.

"I think it's time for my new *friends* and me to leave," he said. "Come on, guys!"

CHAPTER 3

SUPER SYNC SOUND!

In Marucho's room, the brawlers were watching a TV show on the big screen. A woman wearing glasses was talking into a microphone.

"Hi, and welcome back!" she said. "We bring you tonight — the ultra hip Jenny and Jewls Super Sync Sound Extravaganza!"

An audience screamed as two teenage girls bounded onto the stage. Lights twinkled behind them like stars. One of the girls had long, violet hair, and wore a purple and white polka dot shirt over a yellow skirt. The other girl had blue hair and brown eyes and wore a white dress with pink sleeves.

"Whoa!" Dan said. "Jenny and Jewls?"

"Hi y'all," said Jenny, the violet-haired girl. "We're here to hop with our super pop cause we don't stop."

"Or miss a beat, 'cause we are hot," said blue-haired Jewls.

"We're Jenny and Jewls, Super Sync Sound!" they said together, and the crowd went wild.

"That Jenny is so cute, she even makes listening to them bearable," Dan said.

Marucho had a dreamy look in his eyes. "Ah, Jewls, no voice is quite as beautiful as yours."

Shocked, Dan turned to face Marucho. "Are you completely wacked out? The group is totally trash without Jenny."

"You're crazy!" Marucho protested. "She doesn't even do her own singing, she lip-synchs to a soundtrack that plays along."

The boys growled angrily at each other. Runo sighed. *This is gonna take awhile!* she thought.

On the screen, Jenny and Jewls were talking to the TV reporter.

"Okay now, tell us what really inspires you the most," the reporter asked.

"Bakugan!" the girls said at once.

"Bakugan?" asked the confused reporter.

"*Yah-haw!* Bakugan is the coolest," Jenny said. "Why, it's all over the news."

"Uh, yeah, I knew that," the reporter lied.

Dan was impressed. "What? They play Bakugan too? They must be like the total best."

"Yeah — the best girl players," Marucho added.

"WHAT!" Runo yelled.

The boys turned to stare at her. Runo's face was bright red with rage.

"You don't even *know* them but you're calling them the best? That's rich!" Runo cried.

"Uh-oh," said Dan and Marucho. Luckily, a butler in a suit showed up at Marucho's door at just that moment.

"Excuse me," he said, in a British accent. "Refreshments for your overheated friends, sir?"

Marucho nodded. "Follow me," he told Dan and Runo. "There's a full spread, if you're up to it."

Dan licked his lips. "My stomach is ready to rumble. Let's go."

They walked down a long hallway, turned a corner — and stopped.

"Huh?" Marucho asked.

A blue Bakugan was walking across the hallway, dragging jewels behind him. It was Preyas, of course.

"Must keep moving! Must stay focused," Preyas said,

sweating and straining under the load. "Can't stop moving!"

Dan, Runo, and Marucho stared at the strange Bakugan. What on earth was he doing?

"Must move! Must move!" Preyas chanted. "Must — must rest before exhaustion!"

Preyas stopped to take a break. "Hmm. I have the strange sensation that I'm being watched."

Preyas turned his head to see the three brawlers standing there.

"Oh! Abort mission!"

He closed up his Bakugan ball. "Maybe they don't see you. Yeah . . . yeah. That's it! Just don't look. Remain in the stealth position. Ohhhh, maybe I should just take a peek. Act casually, and no one will notice."

Preyas began to whistle, trying to act cool.

"Is that Bakugan whistling?" Runo asked, puzzled. She, Dan, and Marucho leaned over to get a closer look.

Preyas panicked. "Oh no! I've been spotted!"

"And what is it doing wearing all that jewelry?" Runo wondered.

Preyas opened up the Bakugan ball. "Ugh. Fine!" Then he began to talk in a voice like a space alien. "Take-me-to-your-leader."

"Our leader?" asked the confused friends.

"Yes, your leader," Preyas said. "I'm willing to negotiate. I am Aquos Preyas!"

Across town, Jenny and Jewls had left the TV studio. They rode in the backseat of their stretch limo. Their manager, a stern-looking woman in a suit, was driving.

"I'm tired!" Jenny complained, stretching out on the seat. "I wanna play Bakugan. I'm bored at work."

"Yeah, let's ditch all this and go play Bakugan," Jewls agreed.

"Look, I don't wanna hear anymore about Bakugan," their manager snapped. "Until you two clowns are paid for it, zip it."

"Fine!" Jenny and Jewls replied, pouting.

The limo pulled up to a mega mall, where crowds of fans were waiting for Jenny and Jewls to make an appearance. The manager opened the door for them and Jenny and Jewls stepped out, waving and saying hi to the crowd.

"Clear the way!" barked the manager to the mall security guards. "Keep them all back. Shove a little. Use some force, pipsqueak! Don't just stand there."

A smooth, cool voice rose over the noise of the crowd.

"Jenny and Jewls . . . I am Masquerade!"

"Huh?" the girls wondered.

"Over here to the right," Masquerade said, and the girls looked left.

"No, that's your left," Masquerade said. The girls looked one way, then another. "No, the *other* right! Argh!"

"Your right or mine?" Jenny asked Jewls.

"Uh, I think ours?" Jewls guessed.

"Yeah, right," Jenny agreed.

Finally, the girls spotted Masquerade in the crowd. The brawler had yellow hair and wore a blue mask over his eyes.

"Would you ladies care for some Bakugan action?" Masquerade asked. His lips did not move at all.

"But our manager won't let us," Jenny whined.

"Oh, she'll do it!" Jewls said, jumping up and down with excitement. "As long as we get paid."

"Oh, Jewls, you are so smart. She'll totally say yes. She *never* turns down money," Jenny said.

Masquerade smirked smugly.

The girls were just the bait he needed to trap Dan and his friends!

CHAPTER 4

TWO DUELING DIVAS

arucho, Dan, and Runo took Preyas back to Marucho's room. Meanwhile the butler wheeled in tables loaded with plates of delicious food. Preyas sat on Marucho's desk, checking out Drago and Tigrerra.

"Well, look what the cat dragged in," Preyas said. "Draggin-on and Tiger-puss!"

Drago was insulted. "*Draggin*-on?"

"Don't ever call me Tiger-puss," Tigrerra said firmly.

Dan shoved some sushi into his mouth. "Hey man, this is wicked!" he said while he munched.

"Yeah, really great grub!" Runo agreed. "But what's a Bakugan doing crashing your party?"

"Oh, I was just, um, taking a look around, and I

thought I'd drop in," Preyas said. "You don't mind, do you, Muchacho?"

"That's *Marucho,*" Marucho corrected him.

"You have a different way of talking than other Bakugans do," Dan pointed out.

"Well, I'm no stranger to town," Preyas said. "I've been here about six months now, so I've been around the block quite a few times. But I won't bore you with the details. Actually, there was this one really funny story. These creatures, with these claws, they had me up a tree, and —"

"Excuse me, sir." The butler stepped into the room. "Sorry for interrupting your *fascinating* story, but you have further guests to attend to."

Marucho spun around in his chair.

"For me?" he asked.

Jenny and Jewls walked through the door.

"Hey boys, we're here to say, we wanna brawl with just YOU today," Jenny said.

"So get ready, cause we're here to play," said Jewls.

The girls twirled around, then pressed their palms together like they were posing for a picture.

"We're Jenny and Jewls, Super Sync Sound!"

Marucho's blue eyes widened. "Wow! Super Sync Sound are at my party!"

The singers each held up a Bakugan ball.

"Let's throw a Bakugan block party!" Jenny cried.

"So you guys feel like brawlin'?" Jewls asked.

Dan quickly pulled two Bakugan balls from his pocket. "Any place! Any time! I'm ready to roll!" he boasted. He raised his arms above his head, holding a Bakugan in each hand. "I'll warn you now . . . I am one of the best. My name is Dan and I take no prisoners — well, not yet."

Runo growled in frustration. *"ERR!* I only have one warrior." If she wanted to join the battle, she'd need at least three Bakugan.

"'Tis unfortunate, madam," Tigrerra agreed.

Dan looked down at Marucho. "Well now, this is it. Ready to rock and roll, Marucho!"

Marucho nodded. "Yep!"

Minutes later, Dan and Runo faced Jenny and Jewls outside, on the rooftop of the mansion.

"What is taking Marucho so long?" Dan wondered.

Marucho raced up the stairs and outside, breathless. "I'm coming, I'm coming!" he cried.

He ran up to Dan and handed him a white and red Bakugan shooter. This new invention helped players shoot their Bakugan balls onto the field with more power and accuracy.

"Sorry I took so long," Marucho said. "I got these from my dad's factory."

"Whoa!" Dan cried. "Let's try this puppy out."

He strapped it to his wrist. Marucho had a blue and white one for himself.

Dan practiced aiming the shooter on the field. "Runo, check this out!"

"Stop goofing off!" Runo warned.

"Don't worry," Marucho said. "We've got another one lined up for you when you're ready to brawl."

"Yeah!" Dan cried, holding up his arm. "Well, you and I might not need our shooters either considering the advantage. It wouldn't be fair."

"Yoo hoo!"

Jenny held up a finger, scolding.

The girls held up their arms. They each sported a brand new Bakugan shooter.

"Oh, what luck!" Jenny said innocently. "We brought ours too!"

They crossed their arms in front of them, striking a fierce battle pose. Then Jenny grinned. There was a mischievous gleam in her eyes. She held up a Bakugan card with a black background and a sinister skull on it.

"So boys, care for a friendly game of cards?"

Dan gasped. "That's the Doom Card!"

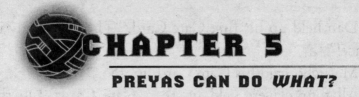

CHAPTER 5

PREYAS CAN DO *WHAT?*

So Masquerade is behind this?" Marucho asked.

"Let me think," Jenny said. "Hmm. Yes, come to think of it, he *did* give me this card!"

"I should have guessed you were up to something phony!" Runo yelled, her eyes flashing with anger. "It matches perfectly with your sellout image."

Dan was stunned. "How could you be so incredibly stupid? Don't you realize you're just puppets to Masquerade?"

Jenny and Jewls looked a little confused.

"Puppets? I don't think so," Jewls replied. "This was a mutual business transaction."

"Yah, we're being paid to bust our moves," Jenny added.

Dan held up his first Gate Card. "Then get ready to dance!"

Marucho held his Gate Card up, too. "Yeah!"

All four players held up their Gate Cards. On the backs of the cards, the symbols of the six planets of Vestroia began to glow.

"Field Open!" the four brawlers yelled.

Bright colors swirled overhead as time stopped around them and the Bakugan field formed on the roof.

Jenny and Jewls each had a Doom Card. They both threw the cards onto the field.

"Doom Card Set!" the girls yelled.

The cards sank into the glowing floor of the field.

Next, the brawlers tossed their Gate Cards onto the field, face-down.

"Gate Card Set!"

The four cards joined on the floor of the field to form a large rectangle.

"Now let's start brawlin'!" Jewls cheered. "Bakugan Stand!"

She used her shooter to aim a brown Bakugan ball onto the field. It landed on the Gate Card in front of Marucho.

"Perfect bull's-eye!" Jewls boasted.

The ball opened up, and the warrior inside transformed into its true form. This beast was a Subterra Stinglash — a wicked-looking scorpion with a human face.

Marucho jumped back nervously. "What's up with Stinglash?" he wondered. He pressed some buttons on the Baku-pod on his wrist.

"Current power level 290 Gs, no other data available," the computer told him.

Marucho thought quickly. *On the battlefield, the Bakugan with the most Gs won the brawl.* "Okay, at power level 300 Gs, let's give Preyas a spin."

He opened his palm to reveal Preyas's blue Bakugan ball. The ball opened up.

"Is my nap over already?" Preyas asked.

Marucho had more strategy to work out. He knew that Jenny had aimed her Bakugan well. When the Gate Card turned over, it would probably raise the Gs of her Subterra Bakugan. But he could use an Ability Card to help him win the numbers game.

"Let's see," he said. "The opponent's attribute is Subterra, so I'll pick —"

"Whoa, Muchacho!" Preyas stopped him. "We don't need an Ability Card. I got some tricks of my own to play."

"So you have a plan?" Marucho asked.

"Of course I do!" Preyas replied. "I plan on winging it."

Marucho looked panicked. "Winging it? Think that'll work?"

"Like a charm," Preyas said confidently. "Just stand back and watch the magic."

He closed up his ball. Marucho loaded him into the shooter chamber.

"All righty then! Prepare yourselves for battle!" Marucho cried. "Bakugan Brawl!"

He thrust his arm forward, shooting Preyas's ball onto the field. It landed right where Marucho wanted it — on the same Gate Card as Stinglash. Now the two warriors could battle.

"Preyas Stand!" Marucho commanded.

The ball popped open, and Preyas transformed into his true form. His blue and purple body was covered in scales, like some kind of sea creature. He had a long tail and claws for hands and feet. His red eyes glowed and he grinned, revealing a mouthful of shark-like teeth.

"Aquos Preyas has arrived!"

"Wow, Preyas. You sure look awesome!" Marucho said proudly.

Preyas laughed. "Get ready, kiddies, cause it's showtime!"

He opened his arms wide, and a fan-like fin popped up on top of his head. Now he looked more goofy than dangerous."

"Uh, maybe I spoke too soon," Marucho said.

"Okay, pick a card, any card!" Preyas boomed. "Don't show me! I love a surprise."

Jewls giggled. "Nice clown act," she said. "But will he drop the ball on my Gate Card? Attribute, coming right up!"

"Great! We have a volunteer," Preyas said, sounding like a game show host.

Marucho almost couldn't bear to look. What was Preyas up to?

"Now if you'll excuse me," Preyas said. He jumped up into the air. His body glowed with rainbow-colored light. "I'll just chaaaaaaaange —"

The light faded, and Preyas landed back down on the field. Now his skin was brown and tan — the colors of a Subterra Bakugan.

"— into something more comfortable!" Preyas finished. "Offer void where prohibited. Some conditions apply."

"What! He changed his attribute to Subterra?" Marucho couldn't believe it.

"Impossible!" Dan cried.

Drago floated up beside Dan. "It's not unheard of but I've never seen it before," he explained. "The Preyas species is known for changing its attributes."

Preyas stretched his arms. "Ah, that feels better. Much better!"

Jenny and Jewls were even more shocked.

"How can it go from Aquos to Subterra attribute?" Jewls wondered. "This clown is some sort of tricked-out chameleon!"

The Gate Card flipped over. Just as Marucho suspected, the card gave a boost to Subterra Bakugan.

"Power increase by 150 Gs on both teams," his Baku-pod announced.

"Noooo! How can his power level be increasing?" Jenny wailed.

Preyas ran toward Stinglash with a karate cry.

"Hiiii-yaaaah!"

He jumped in the air, somersaulted, and slammed right into Stinglash! The battered Bakugan transformed back into a ball and rolled back to Jewls's feet.

"Oh yeah!" Preyas cheered. Jewls looked furious.

Preyas gave the girls a little wave. "Thanks, ladies," he

said. "I could not have picked a better card myself. Now if you'll excuse me, ta ta!"

He rolled back into a ball and bounced into Marucho's hand. The ball was blue again. The attribute change had only lasted for one turn.

"Thanks, Preyas. You were great!" Marucho said.

"Great? I was awesome!" Preyas replied.

Jenny stepped forward. "All right," she said. "The show is over. Time to get back to business!"

"Bring it on!" Dan shouted back.

CHAPTER 6

INTO THE DOOM DIMENSION

"Time to get busy," Jenny said. "Bakugan Brawl!"

She put a blue Bakugan ball into her shooter. It flew out onto the field and landed on a Gate Card. Then Jenny winked at Dan.

"Ready to battle, Danny?"

Dan couldn't help blushing. But he had to forget Jenny was a singing star. He had a battle to win.

"Aquos Fear Ripper, Stand!" Jenny shouted.

The blue Bakugan ball opened and Fear Ripper took his true form: a large creature with long, sharp claws and red, glowing eyes in a sinister face. Plates of blue and aqua armor covered his body.

"Okay," Dan muttered to himself. "Her Fear Ripper is sitting at 300 Gs. But I have a sneaky feeling she's hiding a card and is gonna crank it up."

"Are you going to battle or what?" Jenny asked impatiently.

"Yeah, yeah, just chill," Dan replied. He tossed out a red Bakugan ball. "Bakugan Brawl!"

The ball landed on a card in front of Jenny and Jewls. "Bakugan Stand!" Dan yelled.

The warrior transformed into Pyrus Falconeer. He had the face of a raptor, wide, red wings, and red feathers all over his body. Falconeer had 300 Gs, just like Fear Ripper.

"Don't tell me that's your best move?" Jenny said, giggling.

"You ain't seen nothing yet," Dan promised.

"Hey, it's your funeral, boy!" Jenny taunted him.

Jewls rolled her eyes. "I think he's playin' you, Jen."

"Oh please," Jenny said. "Like you could do better."

Jewls pointed at Marucho. "Hey, there, you ready to party?"

Now it was Marucho's turn to blush. But he was worried, too. What did Jewls have planned next?

"Bakugan Brawl!" Jewls yelled, shooting out a brown Bakugan ball. "Get out of the way, bud!"

The ball landed right in front of Falconeer. "Saurus Stand!"

The ball opened up and transformed into a Subterra Saurus.

"Oh no!" Marucho cried. Saurus was one tough brawler.

"*Battle Status — Saurus at 320 Gs, Falconeer at 300 Gs,*" Dan's Baku-pod reported.

"Watch this, Marucho," Dan said confidently. "Gate Card Open!"

The card underneath the two Bakugan flipped over.

"*Falconeer power increase,*" said the Baku-pod.

Dan pumped his fist in the air. "Now you're mine!"

Jenny grinned. "Ability Card Activate!" She held up a card. "Time to combine Subterra and Aquos!"

The special card gave extra power to Jewls's Bakugan.

"*Saurus to 420 Gs.*"

"Oh snap!" Dan cried. "I'm gonna be creamed!"

Saurus slammed into Falconeer. The Pyrus Bakugan went flying over the field. A hole of glowing purple light opened up above the field. It sucked Falconeer inside!

Dan couldn't believe it. "It's gone!"

"Ah, too bad," Jewls said, but she didn't sound sorry at all. "It must be harder to take when you're beaten by a girl!"

All Dan could think about was his Falconeer, lost to the Doom Dimension forever. That Doom Card was the worst!

The divas did a happy little dance. "We win, you lose! We win, you lose!"

Jewls teased, "Sorry you lost, Danny."

Dan was fuming. "I can't believe they sent my Bakugan to the Doom Dimension!"

"That is true, but you let your guard down," Drago reminded him.

Marucho was busy trying to figure things out. He knew about the powers of the six worlds of Vestroia. Some of the planets had special relationships with each other that played out on the battlefield.

"Now I get it," he said. "By diagonally combining the attributes of their Aquos and Subterra Ability Cards, they simply overpowered you."

"And that means they blocked me from combining the powers of my Bakugan, leaving me a sitting duck!" Dan realized. He turned to his friend. "You knew? So why didn't you tell me, Marucho?"

Preyas floated up in front of Dan's face and started bumping into his forehead. "Hey, simmer down, mister, or I'll have to show you who's boss around here."

Annoyed, Dan tried to swat Preyas away.

"There is a solution," Drago said calmly. "Preyas has the ability to change attributes on his own."

Marucho nodded. "Drago's right, Dan! If Preyas changes into Subterra mode, then he'll be in a diagonal relational with Aquos, which is *me*."

Dan understood. "And if he changes to Darkus mode, then he aligns with Pyrus, which is *me!*"

"Now you've got it!" Preyas said brightly.

Marucho felt more confident now. "This isn't over. We can do this!"

He shot out another Bakugan onto the field. It landed on the only empty Gate Card left.

"Juggernoid Stand!" Marucho yelled. Blue light flashed, and the ball transformed into what looked like a massive turtle with a tough, armored shell.

Then Marucho held up a card. "Ability Card Activate! Water Refrain!"

Blue, watery light appeared on top of Juggernoid.

"According to my calculations, no one else will be able to use an Ability Card," Marucho said. "Thus blocking them from activating their attributes diagonally!"

"Oh yeah?" Jenny called out in a taunting voice. "Watch! Gate Card Set!"

She threw a new Gate Card out onto the field, and then tossed out another Bakugan. The ball landed on the card next to her Aquos Fear Ripper.

"Garganoid Stand!" Jenny yelled.

The Bakugan transformed into a blue creature with leathery wings, a fierce face, and horns on top of its head. Jenny and Jewls high-fived.

"We rock!" they cried.

"Daniel, look!" Drago said urgently. "There are two Aquos Bakugan pitted against each other."

"Then that means — Tsunami! Their combined powers created a Tsunami Wave!" Dan cried.

"It could be even worse if they engage their Aquos Siege," Drago pointed out.

Dan was starting to worry. Unless he and Marucho could counter that move, they were about to be wiped out!

CHAPTER 7

NOT THE BRIGHTEST BAKUGAN

Dan quickly rallied. "Here's the deal, guys," he said. "Our only hope is to defeat them, and the quicker the better."

"No Dan," Marucho warned. "We need to secure our position and make a stand against them!"

"Are you nuts?" Dan asked.

Marucho smiled. "Trust me. I believe my calculations are correct."

Dan scratched his head. "Yeah, okay, I think I know what you're gettin' at so we better get started before we lose another Bakugan!"

Dan threw out a Gate Card. Now there were four Gate Cards on the field again, forming a rectangle.

"Bakugan Brawl!"

He shot out a red Bakugan ball that landed on the empty Gate Card.

"Serpenoid Stand!"

A Pyrus Serpenoid rose up on the card, hissing. Its body was covered with red scales.

Jewls had the next move. She threw down a new Gate Card, then shot her Subterra Saurus right onto it.

Dan smiled at Marucho. "So, seeing as it's your plan — it's your move!"

Marucho wasn't rattled at all. "I believe it's fairly simple," he said. He pointed to the Bakugan on the field. "After all, we have your Pyrus and my Aquos."

Dan looked. Pyrus Serpenoid and Aquos Juggernoid were on the opposite side of the field, on cards across from each other.

"If we add the light attribute Haos onto the battle-field, it will complete our line of defense," Marucho explained. "Fire, water, and light — the Triangle of the Hexagonal Magic Circle!"

"Uh, I am totally clueless," Dan admitted. "But I'm guessing whatever this triangle-thingie is, it'll boost our power."

"Something like that," Marucho agreed. "We just need Preyas. He's our Haos source."

Preyas floated up between them. "Me? You're kidding!

Are you saying you want *me* to go in *there* and risk being sent to the Doom Dimension? No way!"

He stuck out his tongue and let out a crazy scream.

"So, are you all ready to go?" Marucho asked.

"*Noooooo!*" Preyas yelled.

"But we're counting on you!" Marucho pleaded.

"Oh, all right, fine," Preyas said. He closed back into a ball. Marucho shot him out onto the field. He landed on the Gate Card with Subterra Saurus.

"Preyas Stand!"

Preyas popped out of the ball — holding a frilly umbrella.

"Mind if I play?" he asked in a girly voice.

"Be serious!" Marucho yelled angrily.

"Ya mind! This is my party!" Preyas shot back.

A light in his belly began to glow.

"Ooooh . . . change of attribute!"

Preyas jumped up in a blaze of light. He landed back on the card. Now he was dark purple and black.

"What do ya think? Too much?" he asked.

Marucho was furious. "You idiot! You morphed into Darkus! We need Haos!"

Preyas whined like a baby. "I can't do anything right, can I?"

"Hmm. Not the brightest Bakugan," Jewls observed.

"Hey, I heard that!" Preyas yelled.

Jewls pointed to the field. "Gate Card Open! Right now!"

The card flipped over.

"Saurus Power Level Increase," the Baku-pod reported. Dan and Marucho watched as Saurus got a boost up to 390 Gs — more than Preyas, who had 300.

Saurus began to stomp around the card, chasing Preyas.

"Little trouble here!" Preyas called out. "Someone call 911! Hurry!"

Then the protective water bubble disappeared from Juggernoid's card.

"Water Refrain negated."

"What's going on?" Marucho wondered.

"Do something, Marucho!" Dan said urgently.

Then an idea hit Marucho like a lightning bolt. He held up a card. "Ability Card Activate! Time to combine Darkus and Pyrus!"

"Quick!" Preyas yelled, as he raced around the card. "I'm freaking out, man!"

"Preyas, 400 Gs," said the Baku-pod.

"Eeeee-yah!" Preyas yelled. He jumped up and began karate-chopping Saurus all over his body.

Defeated, Saurus turned back into a ball and rolled back to Jewls.

"No way!" Jenny and Jewls cried.

Preyas gave a victory yell and bounced back to Marucho.

Marucho gave a sigh of relief. "Boy, that was too close for comfort. I almost lost my Preyas! Luckily I remembered to link up the Pyrus and Darkus forces at the last minute to pull it off."

"Oh please," Preyas said. "I was in control the whole time."

Dan and Marucho couldn't believe it. "Why you ungrateful little Bakugan!" they yelled.

"A very careless display, Preyas," Drago scolded.

"Hey, lighten up, will ya?" Preyas said. "After all, I did WIN!"

Jenny and Jewls were striking a pose across they field. They looked cheerful.

"This battle is about to end!" Jewls called out.

Jenny threw a new Gate Card onto the field. When the card was set, she shot out another Bakugan. The blue ball landed on the new card.

"Aquos Siege!" Jenny yelled, and a geyser of water spouted from the card. A blue Bakugan emerged from the water. He looked like a medieval knight in blue armor. Red eyes glowed within his helmet. A sword hung around his waist, and a cape flapped around his neck.

"I had a funny feeling they weren't finished with us yet," Dan said.

"I love this game!" Jenny said. "Ability Card Activate! Tsunami Wave!"

A wave of water started to rise up behind Siege. He raised his sword and pointed it at the other Bakugan on the field. The enormous wave swept over the Gate Cards, carrying Serpenoid and Juggernoid with it. The two Bakugan were carried into the purple opening of the Doom Dimension.

Then they vanished.

CHAPTER 8

COUNTER ABILITY CARD ACTIVATE!

There was nothing in the Bakugan handbook about giant waves!" Preyas protested.

"Hey you twisted twins, that's cheating!" Dan said angrily.

Jenny and Jewls giggled.

"Sorry about that, boys," Jenny said.

"Yeah, our bad," Jewls added.

"Present standings — battle tied at one game each," reported the Baku-pod.

There were five Gate Cards on the field, but only one Bakugan standing — Jenny's Siege.

"Time to crank it up a notch!" Dan called out. He threw out a Gate Card. Then he looked down at Drago.

"It's up to you," he whispered. "Bakugan Brawl!"

Drago went shooting across the field and landed on the Gate Card Dan had just thrown. At Dan's command,

Drago stood, revealing his true form — a red dragon with enormous yellow wings and a horn growing from his snout.

It was Jewls's turn next. She shot out a Subterra Centipoid that landed on the card with Drago. The big, brown bug had hundreds of tiny legs wiggling on its long body.

"Gate Card Open!" Dan yelled.

The card flipped over, and waves of blazing fire surrounded Drago and Centipoid.

"Ring of Flames!" Drago roared.

"Do it, Drago!" Dan yelled. "I boosted your power to 420 Gs. And your fire attribute should squash that bug big time!"

The flames leaped higher as Drago grew more and more powerful. With only 340 Gs, Centipoid couldn't win.

"Ability Card Activate!" Jewls yelled. "Hooking up Subterra to Aquos!"

"Oh no!" Dan knew what was coming. The card would combine the powers of Centipoid with Jenny's Siege, giving Centipoid a huge power boost. He watched as Centipoid surged to 440 Gs.

And Jewls wasn't finished. "Ability Card Activate! Attractor!"

"Watch it, boys!" Jenny joined in. "We've just linked up our Bakugan to battle together!"

"Impossible!" Dan watched as Siege walked across the field to stand by Centipoid's side.

"Challenger increase to 530 Gs."

"Sorry, but you lose again," Jewls said smugly.

But Marucho was calm. "Not yet," he said. "Watch and learn. Counter Ability Card Activate!"

Marucho held up Preyas. "I'm betting if I reverse the diagonal relationship and hook Pyrus up with Darkus, it neutralizes their combination attack!"

He popped Preyas into the Bakugan shooter.

"Ready or not!" Preyas cried.

He landed on the card next to Drago, once again holding the frilly umbrella.

"Oh yoo hoo, Mister Dragon, I heard a rumor you've been looking for a dance partner!" Preyas sang.

"You're wearing on me, Preyas," Drago warned.

Jenny and Jewls pouted angrily.

"Hey! No fair! Since when is it okay for Preyas to crash the party? Don't you know it's against the rules?" Jenny said. "I want to launch an official protest!"

Jewls checked her Baku-pod. "According to the rules, they can use a diagonal move to counter attack."

"Nooo!" Jenny wailed.

Preyas grinned. "I'm such a little stinker!"

He jumped up, glowing. "Change attribute! Darkus!"

He quickly transformed and landed back down next to Drago. The flames quickly grew hotter and wilder as the increased power boosted both Bakugan.

"It's working!" Marucho cried.

"Sensing Power Surge."

And there was more power to come. Dan held up a card. "Ability Card Activate! Boosted Dragon!"

The two singers screamed in fright.

"This is worse than a bad hair day!" Jewls moaned in complaint.

"Combined power to 1020 Gs."

A destructive blast of fire burst from Drago's mouth, engulfing Siege and Centipoid. There was a burst of thick black smoke as the two Bakugan balls returned to their owners.

"Yeah!" Dan and Marucho cheered.

Jenny and Jewls frowned.

"At least we're popular," they said.

The Bakugan field vanished around them. They were back on the roof of Marucho's mansion. Runo rushed up to them.

"So tell me guys, did you win?" she asked.

Dan nodded proudly. Marucho turned to Jenny and Jewls.

"I know you love the game, girls, but if you ask me, battling for that creep Masquerade is not the smartest thing in the world to do," he said.

Jenny ignored Marucho and looked at her Baku-pod. "Yo yo girl, we've got to roll!"

"That's right," Jewls agreed. "I completely forgot about it."

"We've got a show tonight!" the two superstars cried. They raced across the roof to the nearest door. "Super Sync Sound Extravaganza rocks! See ya! Wouldn't want to be ya!"

CHAPTER 9

DRAGO'S TALE

The friends watched Jenny and Jewls leave. Then they went back to Marucho's room to tell Julie and Alice what had happened. The two girls were on the big screen. Marucho and the others sat around Marucho's desk. Their Bakugan were perched on the table.

"I fully realize my understanding of your language is limited, however, I do believe the word for those two would be *flakes*," Drago said.

"But they were mildly amusing creatures to say the least, Drago," Tigrerra added.

"What concerns me is the one you call Masquerade," Drago said, his voice serious.

Preyas waved his arms. "If you ask me, I say we challenge that varmint to a showdown!"

Dan kind of liked that idea. "Well, Drago, what do you think?"

"I believe now is the right time for me to explain about the universe I come from," Drago said calmly.

"You mean Vestroia, right?" Dan asked.

"The place where all Bakugan come from," Runo added.

"That is correct," Drago said. "Vestroia is a vast dimension made of six worlds. In the very center of the universe there are two cores. Infinity Core, the source of all positive energy, and the Silent Core, the source of all negative energy. These two cores kept the balance in our dimension."

Everyone listened as Drago continued his story.

"But there was one Bakugan, who, in his lust for control, schemed to grab all of the power for himself," Drago went on. "This had never happened in our universe before. His name was Naga. His mission was to seize the power of the universe. But he didn't succeed. He released all of the negative energy. And now, it has spilled into your world!"

Preyas rolled across the table, excited. "And nobody lived happily ever after. That's it. Bye bye!"

Dan gasped. "Oh man, this is all starting to make sense now," he realized. "All those cards must have fallen through some kinda wormhole or something into our world. And everyone who found them thought they were some kind of game. Boy, were we ever wrong!"

"No kidding!" Preyas said. "You think I came here for myself? Before Naga messed everything up, I was just a cute, peace-loving Bakugan!"

Well, not exactly. Preyas had been battling a Pyrus Garganoid in Vestroia when a Juggernoid fell on his head, sending him through the wormhole. But his new friends didn't need to know that.

"The next thing I know, I wake up in your world!" Preyas said dramatically. "I was freaked! My past was a foggy memory. I only knew I had to find the cute-and-cuddly Preyas I remembered deep inside of me. A Bakugan who loved long walks on the beach and a good book."

Marucho was a little annoyed. "Gee, Preyas, that's interesting, but would you mind not interrupting again?"

"Sorry, Drago," Dan said. "Now go ahead and finish your story."

Drago nodded. "After Naga had disrupted our world, and before Bakugan began entering into yours, there was one human who crossed over into Vestroia."

Dan gasped. "A human? You serious?"

"Yes," Drago replied. "And he was the one who showed

Naga how to enter the center of Vestroia. He opened the portal."

Drago's voice grew sadder. "That was the last I saw of Naga. The negative energy took over Vestroia. That's when I decided to enter your world and put a stop to this insanity."

Runo picked up her Bakugan. "How long have you been here, Tigrerra?"

"Just after Drago left Vestroia, I followed," Tigrerra replied. "I realized my world was about to collapse upon itself and our only hope to save it was to come to your world."

Tigrerra looked at Dan. "Just before I left, I saw the Infinity Core leaving Vestroia to enter your realm forever!"

"Naga must have summoned it here," Drago guessed. "Now our mission is to return the two cores. Otherwise, Vestroia is doomed."

Dan and his friends were in shock. This sounded pretty serious!

"We must find the human who corrupted Naga's mind," Drago said.

"But who is he?" Dan asked.

"If I remember correctly, his name is Michael," replied Drago.

Julie gasped. "Hang on, you guys!"

She raced around her room. "Where'd I put it? I just saw it!"

Finally she came back to the camera. "Okay, you are not gonna believe this. Check this out!"

She held up a school textbook.

"I hate to break it to you, but that's your seventh grade science book," Runo said.

"Lay off, Runo. I think I know who this Michael is," Julie said. She turned the book around to show the back cover. There was a picture of an old man with white hair and a mustache. "Is this the dude?"

"Yes! That's him!" Drago said.

"That is Dr. Michael Gehahbich, the multi-gazillionaire scientist," Marucho said. "Last I heard, he went missing a couple of years ago."

"The guy's a total geek!" Dan said.

Alice gave a little gasp.

"So, what do you know about this guy?" Runo asked.

"He needs a total makeover and quick!" Preyas suggested. "Before I —"

Marucho grabbed him. "Would you zip it? You're not helping the situation with your lame jokes, Preyas!"

Marucho calmed down. "I know this is going to sound kind of weird, but do you guys think that when this Dr. Michael went missing, he really crossed over into Vestroia?"

Dan shook his head. "No, sounds too far-fetched to me."

"Wait a sec," Runo said. "You think there's a connection between Masquerade and this doctor guy?"

Dan frowned. It was all so confusing. They had a lot of stuff to figure out.

If they didn't, not only would Vestroia be destroyed — but Earth was in danger too!

Suddenly everything Dan thought he knew about Bakugan appeared to be wrong . . . the big question was: What should they do next? And how could he and his friends save one world . . . never mind, two. . . ?

CHAPTER 10

ALICE'S SECRET

Alice said good-bye to her friends and shut off her computer. She walked to her dresser. She picked up a picture of herself and an old man with white hair — her grandfather Michael.

"After all these years," Alice whispered. "Grandfather Michael . . . can you really be in Vestroia?"

She couldn't believe it. Could her grandfather be responsible for everything that had happened? Sobbing, Alice sat down on her bed.

"This is Hal-G."

Masquerade grinned as the face of his master appeared on the wall of his room. It was a sinister face with a long nose and glasses.

"How is my little plan coming along, Masquerade?" Hal-G asked.

"Well, let's say we have nothing to worry about, Hal-G," Masquerade replied. "The more we battle, the more our Bakugan will evolve, and soon the Infinity Core will be ours!"

WARRIOR CLASSES

In the alternate dimension called Vestroia,
Bakugan warriors live on six different worlds.
There are many different classes of warriors, and
new ones are being discovered. On these pages
you'll meet some of these beastly brawlers. Look
for more in the next Bakugan book!

MANTRIS

You'll need more than bug spray to take down this insectlike Bakugan. This warrior's claws are like two razor-sharp blades.

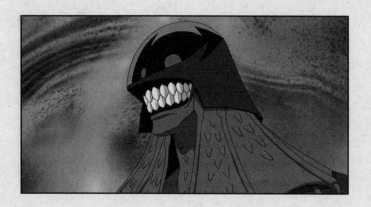

PREYAS

This strange-looking Bakugan looks like a sea creature that stands on two feet. He's got a fishy face and teeth like a shark. But the strangest thing about Preyas might be his unique ability to change his attribute — *without* using an Ability Card.

SIEGE

Like a medieval knight, Siege wears a suit of armor and carries a sword and spear. Luckily, you don't have to be a king or queen to control Siege. If you've got Siege on your team, he'll do your bidding.

TIGRERRA

This magnificent warrior looks like a tiger with razor-sharp claws and fangs. Tigrerra is elegant and sleek off the field, but when it's time to brawl, she will unleash the wild beast inside her.

CYCLOID

Have you ever heard of a Cyclops? This legendary beast was said to be a giant brute with one single eye in his forehead. Cycloid looks like this ancient monster. He carries a hammer in his right hand, and with the right Ability Card, he can bring that hammer down to destroy Gate Cards.

SKYRESS

This winged Bakugan can soar above the field.
Skyress's tail feathers end in spikes. She has the ability
to evolve into a more powerful form, Storm Skyress.

SIRENOID

Sailors used to tell tales of mermaidlike sirens luring them into danger with beautiful songs. The sound of a Sirenoid Bakugan is more like a hideous shriek. But like the sirens of lore, Sirenoids are just as dangerous, especially on the field.

JUGGERNOID

It's turtle time! Juggernoids look like big, bad turtles with shells made of thick armor. You won't find these warriors in a pet shop — they're tough customers in any Bakugan brawl.

HARPUS

In ancient Greece, a harpy was a woman with the body of a bird and the face of a woman. Bakugan in the Harpus class have fierce, fanged faces and large, feathery wings.

Ready for more Battle Brawling Action? Here's a sneak peek at this chapter of the next exciting book, *A Brand-New Brawl*.

CHAPTER 1

A BATTLE BETWEEN FRIENDS

The warm sun beat down on Bakugan valley. Tall cliffs towered over a wide, flat plateau of orange sand. Tumbleweeds kicked up dust as they rolled across the ground.

Two Bakugan brawlers faced off against each other in this deserted battleground. One was a teenage girl with white-blonde hair and big, blue eyes. The other was a teenage boy with straight yellow hair topped by a white baseball cap with a black brim and lightning bolt design. Freckles dotted the bridge of his nose.

The boy, Billy, called out to his opponent. "Hey, Julie! I'm gonna clean the floor with you, and you want to know why? Because me and my Bakugan are a precision team! And we're in the top twenty of the world ranking Bakugan players. Yeah!"

Julie smiled, happy for her old friend. She and Billy

had known each other since they were little kids. They were older now, and they both had something in common — they loved to play Bakugan.

"Wow, cool! Is that really true, Billy?" Julie asked. Every time a Bakugan battle was held, the results of the game were recorded on the Bakugan website. The webmaster, a guy named Joe, calculated the rankings. Only the best players could make it into the top twenty.

"You bet your Baku-pod!" Billy replied. He looked down at the brown Bakugan ball in his hand. "Am I right, Cycloid, or what?"

The Bakugan ball popped open to reveal a warrior with one big eye and a blunt horn growing from its forehead.

"Oh yeah, you said it!" Cyclops replied in a gruff voice. He sounded like a dynamic pro wrestler. "Together, you and me are uuuuuuunstoppable!"

He twisted his head to look at Julie. "So you might as well go run home to your mama!"

Julie's blue eyes glared at Cycloid. Dressed in a pink shirt, pink shorts, and tall white boots, she didn't look like a typical Bakugan brawler. But Julie was as tough as the Subterra Bakugan she used in battle.

"What? How dare you! I'm not going anywhere," Julie

shot back. She looked at Billy. "I can't believe you actually got a talking Bakugan. Where did you find him?"

Julie's friends Dan and Runo both had talking Bakugan, and now Billy. She wanted her own talking Bakugan more than anything — but she had no idea how to get one.

Billy ignored her question. "Yep, we're a perfect match," he said. He tipped the edge of his baseball cap with his finger. "I hate to say it, Julie, but you're toast!"

Julie's hands balled into fists. "That's it!" she exploded. "Let's brawl!"

Julie and Billy each held up a Bakugan Gate Card.

"Field Card Open!" they yelled at the same time.

The air around them shimmered as the Bakugan battlefield formed. The tumbleweed stopped rolling as time within the field came to a standstill. Anyone who entered the valley now would not be able to enter or even see the field.

The two brawlers threw out their Gate Cards. Julie's landed in front of Billy, and Billy's landed in front of Julie. The two cards touched end-to-end to form one long rectangle.

Billy winked at Julie. "Okay, Baku-babe. Why don't you show me what you've got?"

Julie jumped up and down angrily. She was getting pretty tired of Billy's trash-talking. "What did you just call me?" she fumed.

She tossed a brown Bakugan ball onto the field. "Bakugan Brawl!"

The Bakugan landed on the card in front of Julie and popped open.

"Rattleoid Stand!" Julie yelled.

The Subterra Bakugan took its true form, and a giant snake appeared on the card, hissing at Billy. Its long, thick body had brown and yellow stripes. Sharp spikes stuck out of the rattle on the end of its tail. Two long, sharp fangs protruded from its mouth.

"Try *that* on for size!" Julie said smugly.

"Pretty impressive," Billy admitted. He pushed down the brim of his cap. "Bakugan Brawl!"

He threw out a brown Bakugan ball. It landed on the same card as Rattleoid. "Hynoid Stand!"

The ball transformed into a Subterra Hynoid — a creature that looked like a werewolf.

"Do it!" Billy shouted.

Hynoid sprang across the card, its sharp claws outstretched. Julie knew that if Hynoid attacked Rattleoid now, her Bakugan would lose the round. Hynoid had 310 Gs, and Rattleoid had 300.

But Julie knew just what card to throw next.

"Ability Card Activate!" she cried. "Poison Fang!"

Rattleoid's eyes glowed with red fire.

"Hey, wait!" Billy protested.

But it was too late.

"Fifty Gs transferred from Hynoid to Rattleoid," reported Julie's Baku-pod, a small computer that kept track of the battle. Billy watched in dismay as Hynoid was left with 260 Gs, compared to Rattleoid's 350 points of G power.

"Sorry, I know we've been friends a long time, Billy, but I need to teach you a lesson!" Julie called out.

Hynoid jumped back. If he attacked now, there was no way he could win. But Billy had some moves up his sleeve, too.

"Ha! That was just a warm up," he said. "Gate Card Open Now!"

Hynoid roared as a ring of fiery energy sprung up under his feet. A golden glow shone from his body.

"Hynoid's power level doubled to five-twenty Gs," the Baku-Pod said.

Billy grinned. "Friend or no friend, you're going down!"

Julie frowned. "This doesn't look too good." 520 Gs was a lot of power!

"Go, Hynoid!" Billy commanded. "Take him out!"

Hynoid leaped up and grabbed Rattleoid by the throat with his powerful jaws. The ground shook as the big snake slammed onto the battlefield.

"Ha!" Billy cried triumphantly. "You sure showed *me* . . . nice one!"

Hynoid turned back into a ball and rolled to a stop at Billy's feet.

"Humph!" Julie said. "That was only *my* warm up, smart guy!"

A Brand-New Brawl hits shelves in June 2009!